Penguin

This book is for David, with love

A Red Fox Book
Published by Random House Children's Books
20 Vauxhall Bridge Road, London SW1V 2SA
A division of The Random House Group Ltd
London Melbourne Sydney Auckland
Johannesburg and agencies throughout the world

Text and illustrations copyright © Susie Jenkin-Pearce 1988

1 3 5 7 9 10 8 6 4 2

First published in Great Britain by Hutchinson Children's Books 1988
This Red Fox edition 2000

Printed in Singapore by Tien Wah Press (PTE) Ltd

THE RANDOM HOUSE GROUP Ltd Reg. No. 954009
www.randomhouse.co.uk

Penguin

Susie Jenkin-Pearce

Peppi was a penguin and he lived at the zoo.

He hated his concrete enclosure. He hated the way people leaned over the rails and stared at him.

He hated quarrelling for food at mealtimes.

One morning, Peppi looked around him. A penguin's life is not a happy one, he thought, and he stretched his wings and sighed.

That afternoon a careless little boy dropped something into Peppi's enclosure.

Down,

down,

down

it fell.

It had an orange beak and a black coat and plippy ploppy feet, just like a penguin. But it wasn't quite the same.

'My name is Poppy and I'm a toy,' it said. 'And one that is not loved, for my owner has wandered off and forgotten me already.'

'I'll be your friend, and I'll love you,' said Peppi. And from that moment, the two were inseparable.

One day Poppy told Peppi about Father Christmas, who had given her to the little boy. 'He lives at the North Pole,' she said. 'There are reindeer and polar bears. The sea is frosty cold and the whole land is

covered in ice and snow. I'd love to see Father Christmas again. Perhaps then he would give me to someone who really loved me.'

When Peppi thought of the land of ice and snow, his feathers
began to tingle. Suddenly, he knew that was where he
belonged.

    'Let's fly to the North Pole!' he cried. 'If you want to see
Father Christmas again, you shall.'

    It was a dangerous but exciting plan.

All morning Peppi did
exercises to strengthen
his wings.

Peppi borrowed some extra feathers from a seagull and Poppy tied them to his wings.

When he was ready, he climbed to the
top of the penguin slide and launched
himself off. Whoops! It was no use.
He had forgotten that penguins
can't fly.

They decided to hide in the keeper's fish bucket.
   'When it is taken back to the sea', said Poppy, 'we can jump
out and stow away on a ship.'

So after the next feeding time, the two friends hid in the keeper's empty bucket. Soon they were rattling along in the back of a big lorry. The journey lasted a day and a night. When the lorry finally stopped, the driver was astonished to see two small penguins leap out and run away.

'Which ship for the North Pole?' cried Poppy.
    'Over there,' replied a passing seagull.

Poppy and Peppi were soon
aboard and on their way
across the ocean.

After three stormy days and nights at sea, Poppy noticed that the air was turning colder. Peppi looked through a porthole – there were lumps of ice floating on the sea.

'We're here!' he cried.

Poppy climbed on to Peppi's back and clung on tightly while he
bravely leaped from the porthole. Nothing could stop them now.
   The two friends swam ashore.

'I'll have to go,' said Poppy, tearfully, and her little beak
quivered. 'I must catch Father Christmas before he sets off on
Christmas Eve.'

'Goodbye, and good luck,' said Peppi, sadly. 'I'll miss you.'
Peppi wandered off. He loved the feeling of the smooth
cold snow in his toes and the cool fresh air under his wings.

Very soon he met some polar bears. 'Good afternoon, friends,' he said, politely. 'Can you tell me where the penguins live?'

'PENGUINS! PENGUINS!' cried the polar bears in their loud deep voices. 'What are penguins?'

'I'm a penguin,' said Peppi, proudly.

The bears looked him up and down. 'We've never seen anything like *you* before,' they said.

Peppi began to cry. 'But I know that penguins live in the land of ice and snow,' he moaned.

The polar bears just laughed at him and wandered off into the white mist.

Now Peppi felt very lost and alone. Hours passed, but Peppi could see nothing but the great white waste that stretched on forever.

All of a sudden, he thought he could hear a sound; a lovely jingly sound like little bells.

And there, through the mist, came Father Christmas on his
sleigh. And best of all, Poppy was sitting beside him, waving.
Father Christmas gently lifted Peppi aboard his sleigh.

'You are right – penguins do come from the land of ice and snow,'
he said. 'But they live at the *South* Pole, not the *North* Pole!
I'll take you there.'

Father Christmas drove his reindeer across the wintry sky, over the sea and far away. As they flew over the zoo, Peppi could see all his friends in the enclosure. 'They will never know the frosty sea and feel the cold, arctic wind under their wings,' he said, sadly. 'If *only* they could come too.'

'And so they shall,' replied Father Christmas. For on Christmas Eve he can make wishes come true.

Father Christmas flew his sleigh into the enclosure and every penguin, from the biggest to the smallest, climbed aboard. And off into the sky and across the world they flew to the South Pole.

All the penguins of the South Pole had gathered to welcome them, as if they knew they were coming.

'Here is your real home,' said Father Christmas.

He gave each penguin a special present. 'And this is your real home too,' he said to Poppy, 'for I think you *have* found someone who really loves you.'

And he was gone.